Ten Little Gumnuts

May Gibbs

Illustrations by Vicky Kitanov

Angus&Robertson
An imprint of HarperCollins*Publishers*

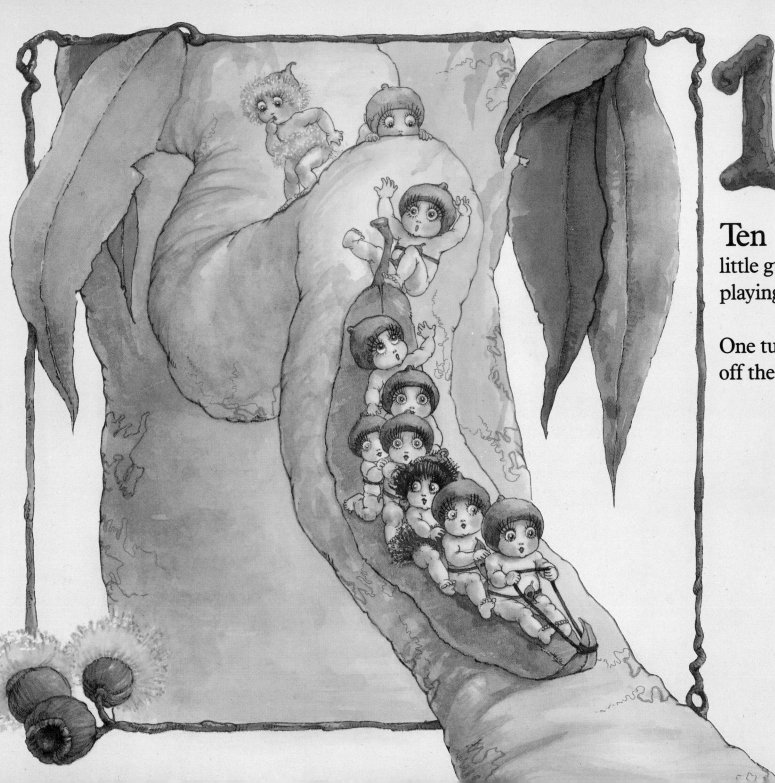

10

Ten
little gumnuts
playing in a line,

One tumbled
off the branch,

And then there
were nine.

Nine
little gumnuts
busy at a fete,

One tried a
lucky dip,

And then there
were eight.

8

Eight
little gumnuts
flying up to heaven,

"Jump!"
yelled Mr Spider,

And then there
were seven.

7

Seven
little gumnuts
playing naughty tricks,

One went
a bit too far,

And then there
were six.

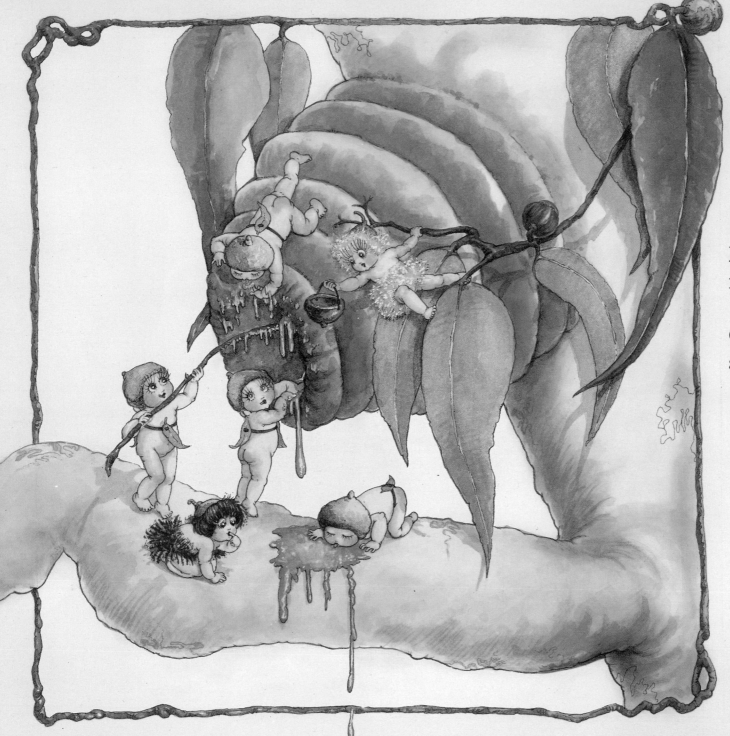

Six
little gumnuts
found an empty hive,

One met an
angry bee,

And then there
were five.

5

Five
little gumnuts
set out to explore,

Alas, they went
a bit too fast,

And then there
were four.

Four
little gumnuts
sailing on the sea,

One found it
rather rough,

And then there
were three.

3

Three
little gumnuts
playing with a 'roo,

One found
a funny friend,

And then there
were two.

Two
little gumnuts
having lots of fun,

One saw a
Banksia man,

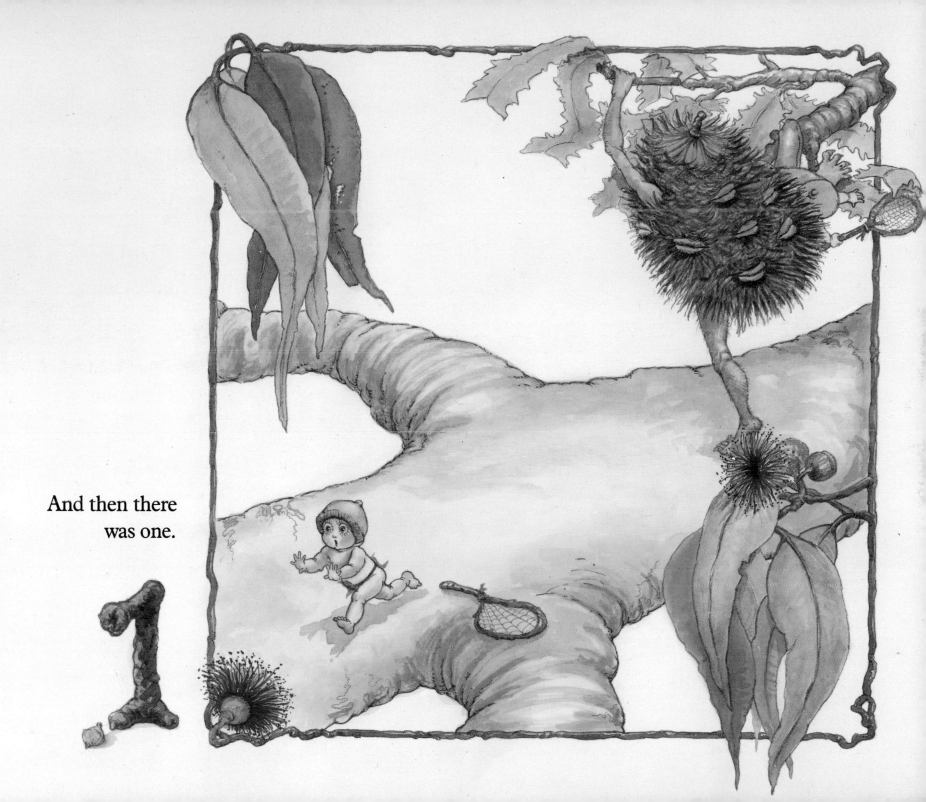

And then there
was one.

1

One
little gumnut
ate a sticky bun,

Then he ate
two lamingtons,

And then there
were none.

No
little gumnuts,
all was quiet then.

Mrs Bear called
"Dinner time!"

And there were
ten again.

10

AN ANGUS & ROBERTSON BOOK
An imprint of HarperCollinsPublishers

First published in Australia in 1990 by
CollinsAngus & Robertson Publishers Australia
Bookclub paperback edition 1990
This Bluegum paperback edition published in 1991
Reprinted in 1992
CollinsAngus&Robertson Publishers Pty Limited (ACN 009 913 517)
A division of HarperCollinsPublishers (Australia) Pty Limited
25-31 Ryde Road, Pymble NSW 2073, Australia

HarperCollinsPublishers (New Zealand) Limited
31 View Road, Glenfield, Auckland 10, New Zealand

HarperCollinsPublishers Limited
77–85 Fulham Palace Road, London W6 8JB, United Kingdom

National Library of Australia
Cataloguing-in-Publication data:

Gibbs, May, 1877–1969.
    Ten little gumnuts. I
    ISBN 0 207 17012 6.

    1. Counting — Juvenile literature.
    I. Kitanov, Vicky. II. Title

513.211

Typeset in Plantin by The Type Shop Pty Limited
Printed in Hong Kong

5 4 3
95 94 93 92